with love

For my grandson Sidney and with love to all my family and friends.

First published in 2011 by Caroline Green
Ganborough House, Longborough, Moreton-in-Marsh, Gloucestershire

British Library Cataloguing-in-Publication Data
A catalogue record for this book is available from the British Library

www.carolinehgreen.com

ISBN: 978-0-9569967-0-1

Designed, printed and bound in Great Britain by
Quorum Print Services Ltd, Units 3 & 4, Lansdown Industrial Estate, Gloucester Road,
Cheltenham, Gloucestershire GL51 8PL. Tel: 01242 584984

Oscar and the Suitcase

Written and illustrated by Caroline H Green

Oscar was not happy. The suitcase had been taken down and was gradually being filled. This meant holidays, and holidays were without Oscar.

So Oscar had a plan.

Oscar sneaked up to the suitcase and took Sam's red shiny spade. Where do you think he hid it?

He took it to the bottom of the garden
and buried it by the poppies.

But the suitcase was still there and
Oscar was still not happy.

So he grabbed Sophie's long stripy
sock. Where do you think he put it?

He wrapped it around his nose and ran as
fast as he could to the washing machine
and flung it inside with the dirty washing.

But the suitcase was still there and Oscar was still not happy.

So he pulled with all his might and out came a pair of Joe's spotty swimming trunks. Where do you think he put them?

Oscar quickly hid them under the bunk beds next to his favourite toy.

But the suitcase was still there and
Oscar was still not happy.

So he flipped Tom's large floppy flip flop out of
the suitcase and balancing it on his nose, ran off.
Where do you think he put it?

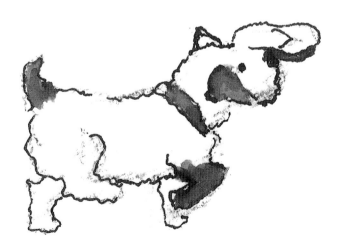

He hid it under
the wardrobe.

But the suitcase was still there, and
Oscar was still not happy.

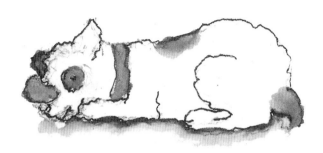

So Oscar took a pair of Mum's sunglasses and
wearing them very proudly he ran into the garden.
Where do you think he threw them?

He dropped them into the pond with
the ducks and the fishes... plop!

But the suitcase was still there, and
Oscar was still not happy.

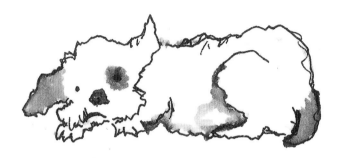

So with one almighty tug he pulled out a pair
of Dad's bright green funky braces and
where do you think he hid them?

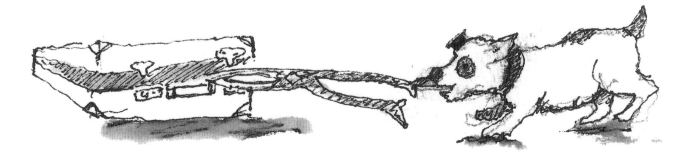

He dragged them to his basket
and pulled his blanket over them.

Then Oscar was happy.

But would Sam be happy?

NO !
He would cry his eyes out if he
couldn't find his bright red spade.

And would Joe be happy?

NO !
He would have to wear his
big brother's trunks and they
would be too big for him.

And would Sophie be happy?

NO !

She would have to wear odd socks.

And would Tom be happy?

NO !

He would have to hop around
with only one flip flop.

And would Mummy be happy?

NO !

Mummy would not be happy
because she would have to squint
in the sun without her sunglasses.

And would Daddy
be happy?

NO !
Because Daddy's trousers would
fall down without his braces!

So Oscar, being the good dog that he really was, brought back Sam's red spade, Joe's spotty trunks, Sophie's stripy sock, Tom's floppy flip flop, Mum's big sunglasses and Dad's funky braces. And Oscar, as best as a little dog could, put all the items back in the suitcase!

And then do you know what happened?

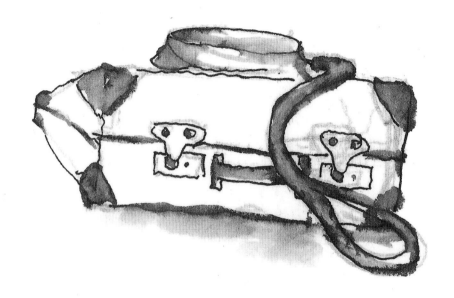

Mummy put Oscar's lead and shiny
food bowl on top of the suitcase

What do you think that meant?
It meant Oscar was going too!

And they were ALL happy.